My Bunny

by James Young

SCHOLASTIC INC. Cartwheel BOOKS®

New York   Toronto   London   Auckland   Sydney

MW01046673

For Emilie
—J.Y.

No part of this publication may be reproduced, or stored in a
retrieval system, or transmitted in any form or by any means, electronic,
mechanical, photocopying, recording, or otherwise, without written permission
of the publisher. For information regarding permissions, write to Scholastic Inc.,
Attention: Permissions Department, 555 Broadway, New York, NY 10012.

Copyright © 1999 by James Young.
All rights reserved. Published by Scholastic Inc.
SCHOLASTIC, CARTWHEEL BOOKS and the CARTWHEEL BOOKS
logo are trademarks and/or registered trademarks of Scholastic Inc.

Library of Congress Cataloging-in-Publication Data

Young, James, 1956-
    My bunny / by James Young
    p. cm. — (Read with me)
    "Cartwheel books."
    Summary: A girl who has momentarily lost her stuffed bunny asks her
father questions about all of the bad things that might happen to it, and he
reassures her that he will always protect both her and her bunny.
    ISBN 0-590-18375-3
    [1. Rabbits—Fiction.   2. Toys—Fiction.   3. Lost and found possessions—
Fiction.   4. Father and child—Fiction.   5. Stories in rhyme.]
    I. Title.   II. Series.
PZ8.3.Y78My 1999
[E]—dc21   98-6931
                                                                       CIP
                                                                        AC

10 9 8 7 6 5 6 4 3 2   9/9 0/0 01 02 03 04

Printed in the U.S.A.   24
First printing, February 1999

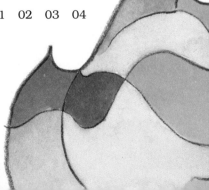

Daddy!
My bunny!
I can't find
my bunny!

Honey, your bunny is
under your bed.

But what if I
lose her again?
What then?

Then, honey, I'll hop
on my horse and ride,
and I will not stop
till she's back at your side!

But what if we're playing
hippity-hop,
and her ears fall off —
ker-plip, ker-plop?

Then, honey, I'll get my needle and thread and sew her ears back onto her head!

But what if a
great, big dinosaur
grabs my bunny
and runs out the door?

Then, honey, I'll search the whole night through and bring your bunny back to you.

Then, honey, I'll search
the starry skies
and get your bunny
away from those guys.

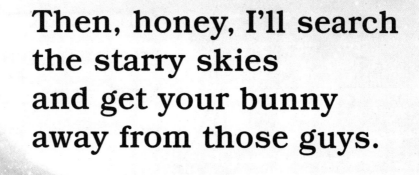

But what about bears
and what about bats?
And what about tigers
and snakes and rats?

Oh, honey, I'll guard you
day and night
and chase those animals
out of sight!

But what if my bunny
decides one day
that she wants
to move away

and go live
with some other kid?
What about that, Daddy?
What if she did?

Now, honey, you know
that can't come true
'cause you love your bunny
and she loves you!

Whatever you do,
your bunny will do.

And, honey,
I love you, too!